SOME
BUGS

SOME
BUGS

words by
ANGELA DiTERLIZZI

bugs by
BRENDAN WENZEL

BEACH LANE BOOKS
New York London Toronto
Sydney New Delhi

Some bugs
STING.

Some bugs
BITE.

Some bugs
STINK.

And some bugs

FIGHT!

Some bugs
FLUTTER.

Some bugs
CRAWL.

Some bugs
curl up in a
BALL.

Some bugs
HOP.

Some bugs
GLIDE.

Some bugs
SWIM.

And
some bugs
HIDE!

Some bugs
CLICK.

Some bugs
SING.

Some bugs do a
BUZZING
thing!

Some bugs
BUILD.

Some bugs
HUNT.

Some bugs
MAKE.

And some bugs
TAKE!

STINGING, BITING,
STINKING, FIGHTING,
HOPPING, GLIDING,
SWIMMING, HIDING,

BUILDING, MAKING,
HUNTING, TAKING—
bugs are oh-so-
FASCINATING!

So
KNEEL
down close,

LOOK
very hard,

and find
SOME BUGS
in your backyard!

For T. and my little bug, Soph, who love all things tiny
—A.D.

For those who encouraged me to play outside
— B.W.

BEACH LANE BOOKS

An imprint of Simon & Schuster Children's Publishing Division • 1230 Avenue of the Americas, New York, New York 10020 • Text copyright © 2014 by Angela DiTerlizzi • Illustrations copyright © 2014 by Brendan Wenzel • All rights reserved, including the right of reproduction in whole or in part in any form. • BEACH LANE BOOKS is a trademark of Simon & Schuster, Inc. • For information about special discounts for bulk purchases, please contact Simon & Schuster Special Sales at 1-866-506-1949 or business@simonandschuster.com. • The Simon & Schuster Speakers Bureau can bring authors to your live event. For more information or to book an event, contact the Simon & Schuster Speakers Bureau at 1-866-248-3049 or visit our website at www.simonspeakers.com. • Book design by Lauren Rille • The text for this book is set in Centaur. • The illustrations for this book are rendered in almost everything imaginable. • Manufactured in China • 0414 SCP • 10 9 8 7 6 5 4 3 2 • Library of Congress Cataloging-in-Publication Data • DiTerlizzi, Angela. • Some bugs / words by Angela DiTerlizzi ; bugs by Brendan Wenzel.—First edition. • p. cm. • Summary: From butterflies and moths to crickets and cicadas, a rhyming exploration of backyard-bug behavior. • ISBN 978-1-4424-5880-2 (hardcover) • ISBN 978-1-4424-5881-9 (eBook) • [1. Stories in rhyme. 2. Insects—Fiction.] I. Wenzel, Brendan, illustrator. II. Title. • PZ8.3.D6238So 2014 • [E]—dc23 • 2013006303

Special thanks to Brendan Wenzel
for creating the perfect backyard microcosmos
and to Andrea, Allyn, and Lauren for giving this book wings —A.D.